Finnigan

the

First edition.

Mary T. Wagner

WATERHORSE PRESS

Finnigan the Circus Cat

Copyright © 2016 by Mary T. Wagner

Interior illustrations by the author.

First edition published June 1, 2016

ISBN: 978-0692679623

Visit the author's website at

www.marytwagner.com

Contents

For my grandchildren
Kai and Reese…

And all my wonderful "grand-kitties"!

Prologue

If there's one thing you can always count on about the circus, it's that there's a surprise around every corner. And for that matter, under every table, in every box, and behind every curtain!

My name is Maximilian—but my friends call me "Max" for short. And I am short. It comes with being a mouse.

And I am not just any mouse. I'm a CIRCUS mouse, and I come from a long and honorable line of circus mice. But...more about the family tree later. Right now, my cousin Leroy and I are still adjusting to the surprise package we just found sleeping under a sweatshirt in the basket on the handlebars of Lucy Farnsworth's pink and white two-wheeler.

As far as we can tell, it's soft, and fluffy, and cute, and it looks absolutely exhausted. And past that, well...we're just going to have to back up the story a week or two.

Chapter One

NEW ARRIVALS

Things had been pretty quiet at the Farnsworth Circus Museum in Beechville, Wisconsin for the past couple of months. Old Man Farnsworth had owned the little museum since before he retired from being a circus clown, and my family had lived here with him for more generations than I could count. We grew up going between the white frame farm house and the big red barn where Old Man Farnsworth kept his five circus wagons and the old daredevil cannon and his trunks full of costumes and other good memories.

He would open the place every Sunday for a few hours and show off the wagons and tell some pretty good stories to whoever stopped by to listen. But mostly he liked to just go down to the stream by the back of the property and fish. And when he got *really* old, he stopped doing even that and just sat on his big front porch instead, drinking lemonade and reading the newspaper.

Well, eventually Old Man Farnsworth took a nap on the porch and didn't wake up and went to the Big Top in the sky.

There never *was* a Mrs. Farnsworth in the picture, so the place has been pretty quiet lately. Until just two weeks ago.

Leroy and I had just got back from washing our faces in the stream one morning. We were stretched out on a hay bale in the barn, right under the east window. That spot is nice and warm in the morning, and its good place for drying out our whiskers before we start looking around for food again. And face it, we're mice. We are *always* looking for food. There was still a whole pantry full of goodies left after Old Man Farnsworth died, so Leroy and I had already eaten a good breakfast of dried apples and stale crumb cake. I was nearly asleep in the sunlight when Leroy gave me a dig in the ribs.

"Hey, did you hear that?" he asked.

"Hear what," I mumbled with my eyes shut.

"I thought I heard a car drive up!" he said. "Didn't you hear it too?"

Now Leroy may be family, but he's never been what you'd call the brightest bulb in the chandelier. And he tends to get a bit nervous when he thinks he hears strange noises.

"Leroy, are you trying to wake me out of a perfectly good nap because you heard a car?" I asked. "We live in town. Of **course** cars are going back and forth." I said. I rolled over on my back and spread my whiskers a bit wider in the sun to dry. Ah, life was good!

"No, really Max, I heard something!" he said. "This could mean trouble! We should hide!"

"Leroy," I replied, "just because once you almost got run over by a fire truck when you were eating a piece of toast in the middle of the street doesn't mean it's going to happen again." I was absolutely positive his imagination was just running wild.

He tugged on my arm. "Max," he said. "Come on!"

I turned away from him...and then I heard the noise too. I looked back at him. Leroy still had that same worried look on his face.

"What are you waiting for?" I said. "Let's go check it out."

We picked a spot at a window that looked over at the house. Leroy wiped a spot clean with his elbow so we could see better. A big blue minivan turned into the driveway. A black pickup truck was right behind it. They both pulled up to the front porch and parked next to each other.

"I wonder what they're doing here," said Leroy. I wondered the same thing. Nobody had driven in here since Old Man Farnsworth's funeral.

A mom and two kids—a boy and a girl—got out of the minivan, and a man stepped out from behind the wheel of the truck. A big short-haired yellow dog followed him out of the truck and started to sniff his way silently around the edge of the yard. The dad stretched his arms above his head like he was stiff, and then reached into the van and pulled out another little kid from some contraption in the back seat. This one was smaller, and he seemed a bit wobbly when he stood up.

"Would you look at that," said Leroy. "People!! Don't they know this place is closed?"

"It sure doesn't look like it," I said.

They all went up the front stairs and looked around the porch and through the windows. We watched as the dad took a key from his pocket and unlocked the door. Then they all walked right in to the kitchen like they owned the place.

Chapter Two

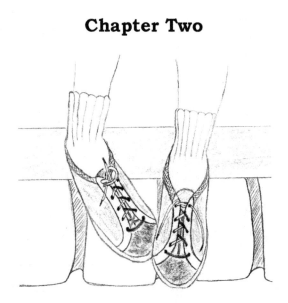

BIG CHANGES

I nudged Leroy in the ribs. "We have *got* to get a closer look," I said, and we both headed to the top floor of the barn. There's more than one way to the house that doesn't involve climbing, but with that dog sniffing around in the yard, we weren't taking any chances. So up we went, under a broken shingle, across the power cable running from the utility pole to the house, then to the tree branch that crossed the cable and up to second floor window, to a tiny hole under the sill.

I squeaked through with no trouble, as usual, but Leroy found it a tight fit. He's big-boned for a mouse. Oh heck, he is **enormous.** He's just about the size of an average rat. Though don't tell him that. He's a bit sensitive about it. Particularly the thing about the tail.

Rats have tails that look like earthworms, all pink and smooth and squishy. Mice don't. We have short, smooth hair on them from end to end, and just the right amount. My mother often told me my tail is one of my best features. Tell Leroy that he looks just like a rat, and he's likely to punch you first and apologize later. Maybe...on the apology.

I don't know where Leroy got his size, but the circus has always been known as a place for folks who are a bit...unusual. Big, little, bearded, tattooed, prone to swallowing swords and fire. So you could say he's in the perfect place for a guy like him.

"You're going to have to lay off the carbs," I told Leroy. He's used to it.

'We could find a bigger hole," he replied, and tugged the last bit of his haunches inside, while his tail trailed behind him.

We stayed on the second floor for a good long time, out of sight and under a dresser. We heard the sound of footsteps clomping up and down the stairs as the kids snooped around and the grownups hauled boxes and suitcases from the van and the truck into the house. The door to this bedroom opened, and the little girl came bursting in. She ran to the window and looked out at the yard. It had a lovely view of the apple tree by the house.

"Dibs on this one," she yelled.

"Cheater!" The older boy followed her into the room and dropped a suitcase and a paper grocery bag. "Lucy, the only reason you got to pick first was that you left your stuff downstairs so you could run faster!"

"Mom," Lucy yelled, "Charlie's picking on me!" She sidled over to the bed and sat down on it. A cloud of dust rose from the quilt.

We couldn't see Charlie's face, but we

could hear the smile in his voice.

"Hah," he said. "You've got the dustiest room in the house. *I'm* going to find something better!" And then he left, stomping loudly down the hallway to the next room where he dropped his bags with a thump. We could hear him walk around, pulling dresser drawers open and opening the window of his room.

Leroy looked at me and shrugged his shoulders. I knew what he meant. The whole **house** was covered with dust. Old Man Farnsworth hadn't been big on cleaning anything but the kitchen and the living room for years, seeing that he usually skipped the stairs to the bedrooms and most of the time just slept on the sofa.

Chapter Three

BOOMER

By the time the sun went down and the moon started to rise on that first day, Leroy and I figured out that things had the potential to be pretty good from here on in.

We left Lucy and Charlie upstairs and sneaked between the walls on down to the kitchen, picking a spot next to the pantry to sit back and watch. The dad—Fred—kept bringing in boxes and suitcases from the car and truck. The mom—Shirley—kept an eye on the little guy as he wobbled around the kitchen. Every so often he'd lose his balance and fall—plop!!—on his bottom, But there seemed to be a lot of padding in his pants and so the only thing that got bruised was his dignity.

After the fifth "whomp" to the floor, however, he finally started to cry. Shirley picked him up and hugged him.

"Donovan," she said, "we are just going to have to find you someplace where you won't get into trouble!" She stuffed him into a high chair, and wiped his face and hands with a wet cloth.

"Oh, look at you!" she said as a coating of dirt and dust wiped right off. "I knew there was a little boy in there somewhere." She poured some dry cereal into a bowl for him and gave him a little box with a straw to play with. Then she turned her attention back to cleaning out the refrigerator.

The dog's name was Boomer. He suddenly pushed through the doorway by the pantry, and sat down next to the high chair. Donovan decided that dropping his cereal on the floor for Boomer to get was more fun than eating it, and Boomer played right along, snapping up the pieces on the first bounce, and sometimes before they even hit the floor.

While Boomer's eyes were fixed on the cereal bowl, Donovan was looking all around the kitchen. I don't know how he did it, but I knew that he saw us. I pulled Leroy closer and tried to push us both further under the edge of the cabinet.

"Hide, you big lummox!" I said in a whisper.

"I *am* hiding," Leroy said. "You don't have to push!"

But still, Donovan kept staring at us. Then he took his pudgy little hand and pointed straight at the pantry!

"Mmmmm......" he said and grunted a little. Oh no, the jig was up!

Shirley looked up from the refrigerator. "Mama?" She leaned over and kissed him on the cheek. Donovan frowned. No, that wasn't it at all. I looked down and saw that Leroy's tail, his pride and joy, hadn't followed the rest of him into hiding but lay out like a piece of string next to the pantry door.

"Mmmmmm...." Donovan said again, grunting louder and pointing at the pantry again.

"More?" Shirley looked at the empty cereal bowl. "What an appetite!" She crossed the kitchen in our direction and grabbed the cereal box that sat right above us. She refilled the bowl and glanced down at the dog. "Boomer, I don't suppose you know anything about this."

She started to clean the kitchen sink. Boomer, who evidently had a better sense of reading Donovan's mind, wasn't so easily misdirected and he walked straight over to us and lay down. He took in a deep sniff with that wet nose. It was close enough for us to touch it. The dog didn't say anything. Leroy turned to me. "Maybe he's friendly?" he shrugged, and put a tiny paw on Boomer's nose. Boomer sneezed. Donovan went wild with laughing, and pointed toward us again. "Daaaaaaahhhhh..." he giggled.

Shirley looked up. "Dog?" she said. "Yes, Boomer is a dog! That's very good!" Then she looked at Boomer. "Hey buddy, get out of there. The pantry is off limits for you." Boomer didn't say anything, just returned to his place by the high chair and waited for some more food to fall his way. I noticed that he kept an eye on us now, and so did Donovan. But as long as Shirley didn't catch on, it seemed like we were in the clear for the moment. Leroy and I snuck back outside.

"That was close," I said. "How could you leave your tail just lying out like that?"

"Well, it just kind of followed me," he said. "It's not like it's an arm or a leg that I can move."

I thought some on that. "Okay, so how about the next time, you just kind of drape it over your arm. Like a purse. Or a towel. Or a cape."

"I like the cape idea," he replied, nodding. I looked back at the house.

"So what do you think?" I asked him. Not like I'd plan to build a space station with his advice, but still, you've got to have somebody to talk to.

"I dunno," he said. "But I think that maybe the dog is friendly. He sure doesn't seem to say much."

I thought on that for a while. I personally am not a very trusting sort. I figure we're too small to take many chances before we figure out who's a friend or foe. Still, the fact that Boomer hadn't tried to eat us or chase us or even bark at us seemed to be a good start.

"Well," I said, "he could certainly help us out with Hector and Godfrey."

Chapter Four

WANTED!!

A "Cat Free" Zone!!

L ater that night, after all the boxes and suitcases were inside the house, the whole family sat on the front porch. Lucy and Charlie carried kitchen chairs out for themselves, while Fred and Shirley and Donovan settled in on the porch swing. There were new pots of red geraniums by the bottom of the stairs now, and Leroy and I pulled up a seat under the wide green leaves. Nobody but Boomer stayed sitting down for long, because the lightning bugs started firing up, and Donovan started to chase them.

"They seem like nice folks," Leroy said. They certainly were *busy* folks, I thought. I tended to agree with Leroy, but like I've said, I'm the cautious one. Plus, I didn't want the fact that I *might* agree with him to go to his head.

"Maybe," I replied. Still, sitting there under geranium leaves with a starry sky above the whole place, it did feel...kind of warm and friendly.

Later, after everybody else—even the lightning bugs—had gone to sleep, Leroy and I went back to the house. There was leftover pizza in the kitchen in a box on the table, and we ate our fill. Cheese, sausage, mushrooms, onions...oh, life was grand! If things kept up like this I was going to have to find a bigger hole for both me *and* Leroy to fit through. We heard the click-click-click of Boomer's nails on the floor before he walked into the kitchen.

"Hide!" I told Leroy, and I ran down the table leg and hid under the cast iron stove. I think Leroy was too focused on eating—go figure—to pay much attention, so he was still sitting there in the middle of the pizza box when Boomer raised his head up to the table top and started to tug the box over the edge. Leroy looked up just as the box was yanked off the table, and made a grab for whatever was closest.

That happened to be one of Boomer's floppy ears, and Leroy scrambled for a flat surface. He found one—right between Boomer's eyes. I thought Leroy was a goner. I put my paws over my eyes. There was no way I was going to watch my cousin become a pizza topping for a dog.

I waited to hear a "crunch"...or a squeal...or something, but I didn't hear anything. I finally opened my eyes again. Leroy was sitting on the kitchen floor, face to face with Boomer. The dog was all stretched out, with Leroy sitting in between his paws and patting him on the nose. I slapped my forehead. "What are you doing? Get out of there!" I hissed at him.

"Look, Max," he said. "We made friends!" Leroy was scratching the stretch of Boomer's face that was just behind his big wet nose, and if I didn't know better, I would have thought the dog was smiling.

* * * *

We finally made our way back to the barn and settled in for the night.

The neighbors started showing up all through the next day, bringing plates of food and stopping to chat. It seems that everybody and their second cousin was curious about what was going to happen to the Circus Museum now that Old Man Farnsworth's family had moved in.

Fred opened the barn doors and showed folks around, taking a polishing cloth to the cannon and telling anybody who would listen that he spent summers here with his uncle when he was a kid. He sounded almost proud of how he nearly set the barn on fire when he tried to light the cannon one day with his little brother inside it. Well that would explain the black scorch marks on the wall behind the cannon!

Lucy helped her mom bring out lemonade and cookies to the barn, since that seemed to be where most of the visiting was going to happen.

Mrs. Applebaum stopped by with her little girl, Cindy. She and Lucy immediately took a liking to each other and went off to explore the wagons. The wagons had been Old Man Farnsworth's pride and joy. There were a half dozen in the barn. A couple more, still pretty broken down, sat in the shed, covered with dust and tarps that were falling apart with age.

Old Man Farnsworth had collected the

wagons over the years, and then tried to fix them up when he retired. They were really old, from back in the day when the wagons were pulled by horses instead of trucks, and before television ruined everything.

When the circus came to town by train in "the olden days," the performers put on a parade to advertise it while the roustabouts were setting up the big tent. Kids and their parents and their friends and their teachers lined up along the way to see the elephants, and the clowns, and the fancy wagons all decked out with gold trim and colorful paint jobs. There were real animals inside the wagons back then, too—lions, tigers, hippos, giraffes, monkeys, snakes. Even now, if you sat inside the King of Beasts wagon with the carved lion heads snarling on the corners, you could almost still smell the lions.

* * * *

When they came back, Lucy had a question for her mother.

"Mom," Lucy asked, "now can we get a kitten?" There was something in her voice that made it sound like she'd asked that question before.

Shirley answered like she'd **heard** the question a hundred times before. "You know your dad's allergic to cats, honey! The answer still has to be *'NO!'*"

"But we could keep him in the barn," Lucy countered. "I promise I'd take care of him every day out there. Dad would never have to touch him!"

Her mother shook her head with a sad little smile. "I'm sorry, you know you can't have a cat around here. Now go play with Cindy." The two girls took their bikes and rode off in a swirl of dust.

Mrs. Applebaum turned to Shirley. "I have a solution for you," she said. "We have a couple of cats at our house. Lucy is welcome to come over and play with them any time. They're quite friendly!" I nearly fell off my seat when I heard that one, but stayed quiet.

"That's going to have to do, then," said Shirley. "My husband can't be around cats at all. If he's in the same room with a cat, his eyes start to water, and he sneezes and coughs like crazy."

"Allergies?" asked Mrs. Applebaum.

"Seems like," said Shirley. "Pretty funny when you think about it, him being from a circus family with all those lions and tigers and other animals in the picture."

"Oh, I know what you mean," Mrs. Applebaum. "My husband comes from a long line of pilots...and he's afraid of heights!"

The two women walked back to the house trading recipes for lemon bars and meatloaf, and Leroy and I sat back and heaved a sigh of relief.

"Boy, we sure dodged a bullet on that one," I said.

"Yeah," said Leroy. "I can't wait until she makes those lemon bars. Can you just imagine the leftovers?"

I swatted him on the back of the head. "About the cat," I said. "They can't have a cat!"

"Oh yeah," Leroy nodded his head, and

I saw that he'd finally landed on the same page as me. The world is a pretty dangerous place for mice. Any number of things would like to have us for dinner—hawks, snakes, foxes, even (ulp!) the occasional dog. But at the top of the list, of course, are cats.

Lucky for us, Old Man Farnsworth never was a "cat person." But that didn't make any difference as far as Hector and Godfrey were concerned.

They might live at Mrs. Applebaum's house and been as pampered as any housecats could be, but they still enjoyed the wild side of things. They usually came lurking over to the Farnsworth place every day or two. More than a few branches of the family tree got picked off by those two, including Aunt Ethel, who disappeared one day when she was out gathering strawberries.

They're the biggest, deadliest, most important reason that Leroy and I have figured out that "overhead" route to the house. When Hector and Godfrey are in the neighborhood, there's just no safe place for a mouse on the ground.

Chapter Five

THE KITTEN

A couple of weeks went by, and things settled into a routine. Charlie spent a lot of time down at the stream fishing and exploring the woods outside the town. Lucy had made fast friends with Cindy Applebaum, and after breakfast she'd pedal her bike the couple of blocks to Cindy's house and the two of them would spend the day giggling together. Or so Leroy and I imagined.

Maybe they spent their time dressing Hector and Godfrey up in doll clothes and having tea parties. Hector was a small, whip-skinny Siamese cat with a brown face and short hair, and he always looked like he'd just pinched his paw in a mousetrap. Godfrey, on the other hand, was *huge*, the biggest cat I'd ever seen outside of a lion's cage. He was the size of a small dog, and covered with a very long and fluffy coat of orange and white striped fur that made him look like a walking footstool.

You'd think somebody built like that would be jolly, or mellow, or friendly, but Godfrey was anything but. He and Hector had been best friends and hunting buddies forever, and you almost never saw the one without the other. The thought of the two of them stuffed into satin doll dresses with lace and ribbon caps playing "Marie Antoinette has a tea party" with Cindy and Lucy had started to be my favorite daydream.

Cindy and Lucy seemed to go everywhere together, side by side. Today was no exception. Except that when they showed up again in the afternoon, Lucy walked her bike into the barn and parked it behind the door, in the shade. Cindy parked hers by the front porch.

Lucy reached into the white wicker basket on the front handlebars, and it looked like she was tucking something in. Then she ran out of the barn and up to porch where she met Cindy. Both girls went into the kitchen, but Lucy looked over her shoulder before she stepped through the doorway.

Leroy must have been having a really great dream, because he stayed asleep and snoring through the whole arrival. I nudged him in the ribs. "Hey, wake up!"

"Ahhh....what's up?" He licked his lips like he could still taste what he was eating in his sleep.

"I don't know, but there's something strange about Lucy's bike."

Leroy looked over the edge of the hay bale. "Looks the same to me," he said.

"No, that's not it," I said. "Look where it is."

"Yah, it's in the barn."

"So?"

"So why is it in the barn? Why ain't it

out by the porch with Cindy's bike?"

"I dunno," he said. "And I don't care. If I get back to sleep, maybe I'll still be in the dream with the cheese curds and hot fudge." He turned over. I was about to let it go, and then there was just the smallest rustle from the basket on Lucy's bike. I strained to hear it, but the sound didn't repeat. Maybe I'd just been hearing things. I shrugged and tried to find a more comfortable spot for a nap. Maybe Leroy had the right idea.

I looked over at Leroy. He was wide awake now, his big ears pitched toward where the tiny sound had come from. He *did* have a thing for strange noises ...when he was awake enough to notice them.

"I heard something," he said. "Did

you?"

I opened my mouth to answer...and then shut it again. We could play the "who heard what" game all day...or we could just go investigate.

We ran down to the floor and up the bicycle wheels until we reached the top of the basket. Lucy had left her sweatshirt in the basket. Nothing moved.

"Do you think there's something under there?" Leroy asked.

I shrugged. "Let's look."

Leroy's the one with the muscles, and so he grabbed an edge of the sweatshirt and pulled it back. Oh dear.

What lay in the basket was small...not much bigger than Leroy. It was damp, and asleep, with its eyes pinched tightly closed. It had a white face and grey striped ears, and a set of white whiskers that were wider than its head. A pair of brown smudges under its pink nose looked like a tiny mustache. It shivered every few seconds, and hugged a sleeve of the sweatshirt that was wrapped in its tiny paws even tighter. It opened its eyes and looked straight at Leroy...and then closed them again.

Leroy pulled the edge of the sweatshirt back into place, and the two of us retreated to the safety of our hay bale to ponder what we'd seen.

"It's a cat!" Leroy said in wonderment. "I didn't know they came so small!"

"That's because it's a baby," I told him.

"He's pretty cute," Leroy said. "And he looks awfully cold and lonesome."

Leroy's got such a good heart. But I

was going to have to set him straight right now. He might be feeling lucky because Boomer had turned out to be friendly.

"He may be all cute and fluffy now, but you know what he'll grow into," I said. I immediately started thinking about where we might have to move to. I hated to leave the Farnsworth place, it had such a bunch of good memories for me. But a cat was a cat was a cat. There was no getting around that.

"Maybe we could be friends," Leroy suggested. "I made friends with the dog," he said.

"Nah, dogs are different," I said.

"How?" asked Leroy.

"Well," I said. "For one thing, I don't think they're as smart."

"What's another?"

"They're naturally friendlier," I said.

"But we don't know if this little guy won't be friendly."

"Doesn't matter," I said glumly. "He'll still be a cat."

At that moment, Lucy and Cindy came back into the barn. Leroy and I picked a perch above the action and hung out. Lucy carried a saucer of milk over to the bike, and Cindy picked the kitten out of the basket.

They took turns cuddling him and watching him drink from the saucer. Then they wrapped him back up in the sweatshirt and put him back in the basket.

"C'mon Leroy, the handwriting is on the wall," I said. "We might as well load up on food for the next few days, because we don't know where we're going to end up."

Cindy finally rode her bike back home, and Lucy spent most of the evening out in the barn. Leroy and I went down to the river bank. Charlie had left the crusts of a sandwich by his favorite fishing spot, and so we feasted on bread and bologna. I never could understand why some folks didn't like the crusts on their sandwiches. They were the best part! Then, when all the lights in the house were out, we headed back to the barn.

Leroy yanked me aside, just before Lucy would have stepped on me in the dark.

"What the heck?"

Lucy was in her nightgown, and she was sneaking into the barn. When she

came out, she had the sweatshirt all
rolled up in her arms. Then as we
watched, she tiptoed back into the house,
as quiet as a mouse.

Chapter Six

THE PLAN

We weren't always circus mice. Way back in the past, more "greats" than I could count, one of my great-great-great (you certainly get the idea) grandfathers was the "pocket mouse" of the royal physician to Mad King Ludwig of Bavaria. That lucky mouse had it made in the shade. He spent most of his time as a pet in the vest pocket of the good doctor's coat, safe, warm, pampered and very well fed.

Oh, to be feasting on the leftovers from the royal household! The beef! The creamy potatoes! The pastries under heaps of whipped cream! You can imagine that my great-great-great grandfather Felix didn't have much incentive to get out and see the world. Life in the castle with the good doctor was very, very good.

But...if my great-great-great grandfather didn't care about getting out and about, that wasn't true for the good doctor. And so one day the doctor traveled to Berlin for a medical conference to learn more about bloodletting and leeches and all the latest ways to tie bandages. As you can imagine, the eats were pretty good where the doctors all gathered. But the circus was in town as well, and after two days of swapping tales about "modern" medicine, the good doctor and his buddies decided to go out on the town and spend a little time at the circus that had just arrived.

As family legend goes, Felix climbed up to look over the edge of his pocket just as the good doctor from Bavaria stepped through the striped canvas walls of the big top, and that mouse was absolutely mesmerized. Hypnotized. Caught, hook, line and sinker.

The music! The excitement! The fire-eaters! The acrobats! The folks soaring on the flying trapeze! The clowns with their baggy pants and the ladies with their sparkly outfits and swirling skirts with feather trims! The lions and tigers in the center ring, as the elephants stood in the wings waiting for their turn. Horses with plumes on their heads racing around another ring, twirling together and dancing as a man stood in the center and cracked a whip, while a lady stood on the back of the biggest horse, barefoot and balancing on one leg.

There was an energy and an electricity and an excitement that hit him like a thunderbolt. And in that life-changing instant, he knew he would never be happy again sitting in the doctor's pocket, listening to chamber music at the castle and nibbling on **schaum torte** off of china plates rimmed with gold.

He scurried up and out of the pocket, ran down the length of the coat and then down the leg of the doctor's pants, and never looked back.

The circus has been in our blood ever since then. Leroy and I sat there in the dark, in the middle of the flowers that he'd pulled me into, and stared up at the sky lit with a full moon and sprinkled with stars. It was going to hurt like crazy to leave the Farnsworth place.

"Let's go inside," said Leroy. "I'm hungry again."

I smacked my forehead with a paw. I really wanted to just go back to the barn and hang out with what were soon going to be only memories. But Leroy is a big boy, and it takes a lot of food to keep up that chunky, rat-like physique.

We checked out the leftovers in the kitchen trash bin while Boomer snoozed by the stove. Chicken and macaroni and cheese for dinner, with some broccoli and chocolate cake for good measure—good grief, why'd we have to leave just when the eats were really getting good? It just wasn't fair! I gnawed on a chicken bone.

"Hey," said Leroy. "Did you hear that?"

All I could hear was the sound of Boomer snoring.

"It came from upstairs," he said. He wiped the last of the chocolate frosting from his paws, then gave his whiskers a quick swipe. "Let's go."

We'd been through this "I heard a sound" thing before. Why argue?

We were halfway up to the second floor, going between the walls, when I heard it too. It was a sneeze. Leroy stopped to listen, and I bumped into his tail end.

"Keep moving," I said, and I shoved his

tail out of my face.

We found our way into Lucy's room and climbed up to the window sill. The moonlight was bright and shone across her bed. Lucy looked like she was asleep, but there was a tiny ball of grey and white fluff curled up on her pillow, nestled right up against Lucy's blonde curly hair. The grandfather clock at the base of the stairs chimed midnight.

"Oh look, Max." Leroy said. "It's the baby. He looks so...sweet!"

If you haven't guessed it yet, Leroy has kind of a hopeful, romantic soul. I could see by the look on his face that he was rapidly becoming enchanted by the unmistakable cuteness of Lucy's new friend. He tiptoed over to the bed and sat there, positively beaming.

I had to admit that if you've ever heard the phrase "there's nothing cuter than a kitten" it would be pretty hard to argue about it now. The kitten's little grey and white striped sides heaved up and down while it breathed. One tiny furry paw was stretched out, and it flexed just a little. Probably dreaming about catching a mouse, I thought sourly. **Somebody** had to be practical here.

Leroy reached toward the kitten and put a paw on its head. "He's so soft," he whispered. "Here, you try it!"

"Are you nuts?" I hissed back, but before I could step back, Leroy had taken my paw in his much bigger one, and made me stroke it. It **was** pretty soft, in fact the softest thing I'd ever felt.

Then just as the last of the chimes

passed into the night air, Leroy lost his balance on the soft bedcovers, and fell right into the kitten's arms. The little guy's eyes shot open and he looked at the two of us. No, he positively **stared** at us. I looked over at Leroy, and saw that he was backlit by the moonlight, with a sort of silvery glow around him. With the moonlight streaming behind us, we must have looked like ghosts or apparitions of some sort.

"Who are you?" the little guy asked in a shaky voice. "And where am I?"

"Oh, that one's easy," Leroy volunteered. "You're at the Farnsworth Circus Museum," he said. "And we're..." He winced as I swiftly kicked him in the knee.

I'd suddenly had an idea, and it was

going to take faster thinking than Leroy usually had the gears for. I stepped a bit closer.

"We're your fairy godmothers," I said. Leroy's mouth fell open with shock, but for once no sound came out.

The kitten stared at us with about as much comprehension as if I'd started reciting the periodic table of elements. "What's a godmother?" the little furball asked. "And what's a fairy?"

I figured it wouldn't be long before Lucy was dressing him up for tea parties and reading him fairy tales, so I didn't need much of a bridge here. Just enough to get us stamped into his mind in a friendly way before he ever met Hector and Godfrey.

"Somebody who makes your world a

better place," I said. "We're gonna watch over you and keep you safe, show you how stuff works," I improvised. "In fact, we're going to be your very best friends."

"How did I get here?" he asked, looking around Lucy's room in the moonlight. I could even feel my own heartstrings tug a little.

Leroy and I looked at each other and shrugged. If he didn't know, maybe it was better that he didn't remember. I couldn't think of an answer right away...and then I didn't have to. The sound of sneezing came from down the hall again. These were really *big* sneezes. They sounded like they came from a horse that accidentally sniffed a pot of pepper. It had to be Fred. Good old allergic Fred.

We heard Shirley wake and ask

"What's the matter dear?"

Fred mumbled something about cats, and Shirley laughed. "Don't be silly," she said. "It couldn't be a cat! Must be all the dust around here."

The sound of sneezing even began to wake Lucy, who had been sleeping as soundly as a hibernating bear. Leroy and I scampered off the bed and hid behind the window frame just as she sat up in the bed and rubbed her eyes.

She looked down at the kitten, who was tangled in the sheets she pushed aside, and then she picked him up and held him close under her chin. He started to purr, so loud we could even hear it from the window frame. It sounded like the burble of a pot full of cream simmering on the stove.

Then the sound of Fred's sneezing continued to cut through the night air. All the noise woke up Donovan, who started to cry. We heard Shirley's bare feet hit the floor and then start to pad over creaky floorboards to Donovan's room, and we figured it was time for us to hit the road.

We gave the little guy a quick wave. Then as long as we were on the second floor, we took the high road across the power cable back to the barn and settled in for the rest of the night. Fred sneezed all night long.

But not before we heard Lucy tell the kitten "I guess you're going to be living in the barn after all. But for tonight, you still get to sleep here with me."

Chapter Seven

FINNIGAN

ALL in a NAME

Sure as shootin', Lucy and the kitten were back in the barn the next morning, with another saucer of cream. Well, it was barely morning. It seemed like the sun was still pulling the covers back up to its chin, and Lucy was still in her pajamas. She made him a little bed out of doll blankets in the hay behind the King of Beasts wagon, then sneaked back into the house and back up to bed.

Leroy and I didn't waste any time.

"So, little fella," I said. Leroy sniffed closer to the saucer of cream while the kitten lapped at it with a tiny pink tongue, but I slapped his paw away from it. "Do you have a name?"

The kitten looked up from his breakfast. "I don't think so," he said. There was cream on his whiskers and a dab of it on his nose. He'd shaken himself loose out of the blanket, and we finally got to see him from stem to stern. He still didn't look much bigger than Leroy.

"We should pick you a good one if you're going to be living here," said Leroy, his eyes still on the saucer. "Hey, are you going to finish that?"

"Yeah," I said, thinking so hard that my brain started to hurt. The bigger problem was going to be how to get Lucy to know what perfect name we'd picked when we figured one out. And let's face it, in the circus world, the right name carries a lot of weight.

Do you think that Jumbo the Elephant would have gotten quite as much press if he'd been named "Skippy"? Would General Tom Thumb, the world-famous midget, have been quite the draw if he'd been named "Alphonse"? Would the Ringling Brothers' great horse Silver King have been quite as famous or glamorous if he'd been named…"Aluminum King"?

Don't be silly!

I kept thinking while I looked the little guy over. He had a face and a chest that were mostly white, with those smudges under his nose that gave him the look of wearing a mustache.

His belly was white too, along with his arms and his back paws. The rest of him was covered with grey and black stripes, all the way down nearly to the tip of his tail. The tip of his tail was white, like someone had dipped a brush in a can of paint. And the whole package was fluffy.

This was going to be a challenge, for sure. And we were going to have to work fast. It wouldn't be long before Lucy and Cindy came back to the barn and started to work on picking a name themselves. Not that they weren't great kids and all but...it would be a tragedy if this new circus kid ended up with a label like

"Fluffy" or "Princess" or "Cuddles."

He finally quit lapping up the cream, and sat back down and stared at us with big green eyes. I had to admit, he was **awfully** cute...for somebody that was going to grow up to be a cat.

Leroy seized his opportunity and moved in on the cream left over in the saucer. I swear, he loves to eat so much that if **he'd** been that doctor's pocket mouse in the court of Mad King Ludwig, circus or not he'd have never left that comfortable pocket and all the leftovers at the court, and none of us would be sitting here in Beechville.

"Hey Max," said Leroy. "Doesn't he remind you of somebody?"

"Yeah," I said. "A cat."

Leroy rolled his eyes. He does that once

in a while when he thinks I'm being dense about something. As *if!*

"Besides that," he said. He slurped up the last of the cream, then wiped his whiskers. "Look over there, behind you."

I turned around. Behind me was the back wall of the barn, with a huge wooden chest and the cannon. It was still dark and gloomy in the morning shadows. "What?" I asked.

Leroy waddled across the barn, kicking up sawdust behind him. Then he ran up the side of the chest, and perched on top of the cannon and held up his arms like a ringmaster welcoming a crowd. I thought he had lost his mind.

"Ta da," he said in a booming voice. "Behold the *GREAT*, the *MIGHTY*, the *INCREDIBLE* ... Finnigan!"

Clearly, there was a thread running through Leroy's mind that I had not caught on to. On the other hand, if I didn't catch it soon, his entire brain might unravel. I followed him across the barn and up to the cannon where he sat. He had turned around to face the wall by now, and was staring intently at something. Just what, I didn't realize until I got there.

There were wagons, and trunks, and other circus props stashed around the barn, of course. But Old Man Farnsworth had also decorated the walls with circus posters from his traveling days. They were faded by now, and some of them were torn or stained from where rain or snow had landed on them. But if you stared at them long enough, you could just about hear the roar of the crowds and smell the popcorn and the elephants, and taste the cotton candy. On the posters, daredevil trapeze artists soared through the air high above the ring. There were posters for lions and tiger acts, dancing horses, snake charmers, and Velma, the bearded lady. And right in front of us, looking like he's just stepped out of the circus train in 1920, was a poster for Finnigan, the world's strongest man.

Even in the gloomy morning shadows that draped that side of the barn, Finnigan the Strongman was a pretty awesome sight. If you actually believed what you were seeing, he was standing in the center ring, hoisting a dumbbell with 500 pound weights on each end. And on top of each weight sat a pretty lady in a ruffled dress and a fancy hat, her legs crossed daintily at the ankles and with a parasol above her head. There were two chains attached to the dumbbell as well, on either side of Finnigan's head, and they connected two more 400 hundred pound weights to the whole thing.

You wouldn't want to mess with Finnigan in a bar fight. His arms bulged with his incredible biceps. He had massive muscles going up and down his legs. His neck looked like a small barrel covered with muscles. He probably even had muscles on his toes. On the other hand, he didn't look anything like a kitten. I scratched my head. What did this have to do with anything?

"Ahem," I coughed gently to get his attention. "Leroy," I asked delicately. "Is there a point you're trying to make here?"

"Yes, silly!" he said. "We should name

the new kid Finnigan!"

My jaw dropped. "What are you talking about?"

I turned around to see that the little guy had followed us across the barn, and was sitting at the base of the cannon. I don't think he'd gotten his "climbing legs" yet. He looked tiny enough to fit in a coffee mug, with room to spare.

I looked back at the poster. "I don't get it," I said.

"Sure you do!" said Leroy, as happy as I'd ever seen him. "They're identical!"

I looked back at the kitten and scratched my head again. I still didn't get it.

"What's up," the little guy asked, his green eyes all innocent and big as buttons.

"Leroy here thinks you look like the guy in the poster," I said. I was about to say "I think he needs to get his eyes checked ..." but then I looked again.

Okay, so they didn't have anything in common in the size department. Or the muscles department. Or the part about Finnigan the Strongman being a human being and the new kid being...a kitten.

But as I looked back and forth from one to the other, I finally got what Leroy had figured out from the other side of the barn.

What was Finnigan the Strongman wearing? A striped grey and black leotard and tights from his shoulders to his feet. His lily-white arms were bare, to better show off his bulging biceps. The top of his chest was bare too, to better show off that rock-hard set of muscles straining to lift all that weight. And under his nose was a luxurious handlebar mustache. It was a pretty sweet match.

I stared at the kitten, who had no idea what we were all excited over and just kept staring at his surroundings.

"We've got a name for you, kid," I said. I pointed at the poster. "It's perfect. It's absolutely circus perfect."

Chapter Eight

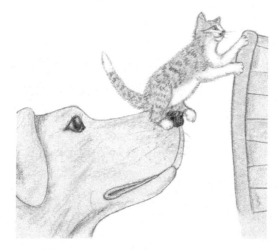

TEAMWORK!

So **WE** had figured out the perfect name for the kitten. Now came the hard part—getting Lucy to figure it out too. Sure as shootin', Cindy arrived around lunchtime, and the two girls ran to the barn to visit their new pet. We'd talked to Boomer earlier in the morning, and he followed them inside as well. Timing was going to be absolutely **everything!**

Lucy scooped up the kitten and held him in her arms. Just like we thought, the two girls started brainstorming for names. "I like Cuddles," said Lucy.

"I think Moonbeam would be a good name," said Cindy.

Oh good grief.

As the sun had passed overhead during the morning, the back wall of the barn (and the cannon, and the poster) had brightened up a bit. In just a couple of minutes, the time would be perfect. As long as Lucy and Cindy hadn't picked a different name first!

First Boomer went over to the girls like he wanted to get in on the action, and started begging for attention. He shoved his big head under Lucy's elbow like he was jealous, and knocked the kitten and the blanket clean out of her lap.

Finnigan—because that's what Leroy and I had started calling him already—took his cue, and as soon as that blanket hit the floor, he started to make his way across the barn to the other side. He stayed under the radar, though, weaving his way through stacks of hay and under the wagons. Lucy pushed Boomer's head out of her lap, and started looking for her new pet. Boomer pretended like he didn't know what was going on, and kept begging her for some hugs.

"Where did he go?" Cindy asked. She and Lucy finally stood up and started looking around. They looked behind the bale they'd been sitting on, but came up empty. Cindy opened a brass-bound trunk next to the wall. The two girls looked inside. "Ooooohhhhh...." they both said together, staring at a pile of silky costumes. They rummaged through the fabric and came up with a tiara, a pair of gigantic clown shoes and a red nose...but no kitten.

Cindy finally spotted him halfway across the barn, and pointed him out to Lucy. The two girls made a dash across the ring, but Boomer ran interference like he was herding sheep, and blocked them long enough for Finnigan to disappear from sight again. Leroy was already perched on a beam above the cannon, waiting for his cue. I ran alongside Finnigan, who was starting to wear out from all the running. Remember, his legs weren't very long yet!

"C'mon, kid," I said, and patted his shoulder. "We're almost there!"

"Are you sure this is going to work," he asked.

I thought briefly about telling him the truth—I had *absolutely no idea whether this would work!* But then I remembered that I'd already convinced him Leroy and I were his fairy godmothers. Why not stay confident? After all, this was the circus, where confidence and illusion could make magic happen.

"Of course it will!" I said cheerfully, and darted ahead of him just as we got to the base of the cannon.

Lucy and Cindy were close behind us, though they just didn't know it. Boomer kept threading himself around them to mess up their progress and give us a little more time to set up.

We got to the saw horse next to the cannon, and Finnigan dug in with his tiny claws to pull himself to the top. Then he collapsed, completely exhausted.

"C'mon, Max," Leroy called from his perch. He had been pushing aside a roof shingle to let in a single beam of sunlight that now fell across the cannon, right under the poster of Finnigan the Strongman. "Let's get going here!" He went back to pushing, and with one final heave a spotlight of sunlight hit the sweet spot, lighting up the cannon and the poster behind it. The only problem was, there was no kitten sitting there.

I tried to nudge little Finnigan to his feet, but he just lay there in a pile of fluffy grey and white fur, all out of breath. I looked at the top of the cannon, and knew that there was absolutely no possible way that he was going to be able to jump to the top from where he was. I looked over at Leroy, and shrugged my shoulders. Yes, usually I'm the one who figures out the next move, but I was fresh out of ideas.

That's when Boomer showed up. He used that big nose of his like a shovel, and scooped Finnigan on to the bridge of his nose like he was balancing a treat. Then he stood up on his hind legs and let Finnigan walk from his nose across the cannon to the spotlight.

"Good dog," I shouted. I could have kissed him. Then I turned to Finnigan. "Hey kid, this is your moment. Make it look good!"

Finnigan sat up straight and proud, even though you could tell he was a bit nervous.

With Fred doing all that polishing, the top of the cannon was a bit slippery. But the little guy held his mark like he was born to the ring, and I felt quite proud of him at that moment.

I waited for the girls to finally notice and catch on. But when I turned around to find them, they had wandered a bit off course again. They had reached the other side of the barn, and were rummaging around the wagons, looking under them and checking behind the doors.

Cindy shrieked when she rounded a corner and suddenly came face to face with a carved cobra head on a corner of the Snake Pit wagon. Lucy had been looking under the wagon, and banged her head as she sat up. *"OW!!"* she said, rubbing the top of her head.

"How long do I have to sit here?" asked Finnigan. "I think I'm going to start melting any minute!"

"Sit tight, kiddo." I said. "It ain't over until the fat lady sings." I turned to Boomer for help.

"Say something!" I pleaded.

Boomer had proven to be a dog of very few words. In fact, in the past two weeks, I hadn't heard him even whimper. Some dogs are like that. Some, on the other hand—like Mrs. O'Leary's schnauzer down the street—can never shut up. In the balance, I prefer the ones who don't make a lot of noise. It wasn't helping us now, however.

"Max," said Leroy from his seat beside the shingle. "Hurry up. We're gonna lose the light!"

I begged Boomer again. "Do something, will you?" He just raised an eyebrow and stayed put. I think he felt his part in the drama was all done.

I looked back for Leroy, but he was nowhere to be found. I smacked my forehead in despair. What the heck was he doing deserting us at a time like this? I looked back up at Finnigan, who was waiting patiently for his big moment.

Lucy and Cindy were still rooting noisily around by the wagons, without a clue. I noticed that the spotlight on Finnigan was already starting to move a little, but the little guy held his place like a regular trouper.

It was going to take a miracle to make this work.

Then I heard a rustle in the hay behind me, and caught a glimpse of Leroy. He was scampering up Boomer's left hind leg. I didn't know that Leroy could move that fast! Boomer turned his head just in time to see Leroy run halfway down his tail, and then sink his sharp front teeth in it.

Boomer let out a pained, giant "**WOOF!!**" so hard it nearly shook the rafters. I was so surprised that I fell backwards, but Lucy and Cindy came running over to Boomer. He looked straight up toward Finnigan sitting on the cannon, in his own personal spotlight, and Lucy and Cindy suddenly forgot all about poor Boomer.

"Cuddles!" cried Lucy.

"Moonbeam!" cried Cindy.

Good grief, they just weren't getting this at all, were they. They began to climb over the stuff and reach toward Finnigan where he sat on top of the cannon, but the little guy was smarter than I'd given him credit for. Despite his precarious perch, he scooted out of reach, right to the back of the cannon and over to the poster, and reached up with both tiny paws like he wanted them to see something. Heck, like he was *pointing* at something!

He could barely make it, but he landed his front paws on the bottom edge of the poster, which was still lit by the beam of light. I saw his back feet start to slip, but before I could even make a move to try to help, Boomer jumped back into the act and shoved his nose under Finnigan's belly just as his back feet slipped out from under him.

The girls' gaze finally turned upwards to the poster.

Finnigan the Strongman stood tall and proud, his handlebar mustache gloriously thick, his muscles upon muscles proudly bulging, his name spelled out in giant fancy letters at the top of the poster...and on the bottom as well.

"Hey Cindy," Lucy said. "Look! The kitten is wearing stripes just like the guy up there."

"What do you think it means?" asked Cindy.

"I don't know," said Lucy. "But look, he's even got a mustache!" She furrowed her brow like she was puzzling hard over something. "Do you think he's trying to tell us something?"

People can be so dense! She finally reached the kitten, and pulled him off his precarious perch on Boomer's nose. Boomer sneezed and shook his head, flapping his dangly yellow ears back and forth.

"Of course not," Cindy said. "Animals just aren't that smart."

Oh, what an insult! I thought about asking Leroy to bite her in the ankle, but I knew that in the long run, it wasn't going to help.

Lucy had brought the doll blanket with, and she proceeded to wrap it around Finnigan again. Finnigan struggled to get loose. It was hard, but he managed to get one little arm out of the folds of the blanket. He stretched out his paw one more time toward the cannon and the poster of the original Finnigan, and made a little "meep" sound. To tell the truth, it sounded more like something coming from a baby chicken, but it did the trick.

Lucy looked down at her new pet, and then back at the poster, and then back at the kitten, like she was trying to sort out something important.

"Well then Finnigan it is, little guy," she said with a smile, and she and Cindy made tracks for the other side of the barn. Leroy came out from where he'd been hiding once the girls got there, and he sank down in the sawdust next to me with a big plop. "That was pretty exciting," he said.

"That's the understatement of the year, big fella" I replied. Boomer flopped down next to us, an annoyed look on his face. Leroy scratched the top of Boomer's nose, and the dog seemed to relax a bit.

"I'm sorry about the bite," he said. Boomer replied by licking him. At least I **hoped** he was just licking him and not tasting him.

"Let's get out of here and down to the stream," I said. "I've had about as much excitement in this barn as I can stand for one day."

Leroy and I made our way past the house, staying under the bushes until we got past the kitchen. Whatever was cooking for dinner sure smelled good, and I knew that once everyone was asleep in the house, we were going to have a pretty good feast.

"Think he's going to be OK?" Leroy asked me as we walked. "He's awfully little."

"Yeah, I think he'll be fine," I said. "You know the circus life, nothing comes with a guarantee...but we got him a good name, and that is *huge* step."

"Those are going to be some big shoes...or muscles...to fill," said Leroy.

"Yeah, I know," I said. "But then he's got two great fairy godmothers to help, doesn't he?"

Chapter Nine

GROWING PAINS

Finnigan grew like a weed for the rest of the summer. That is, if weeds had fur and claws and whiskers. Funny thing is, it seemed like some parts grew more than others.

Now Leroy and I lived what you might

call a sheltered life when it came to cats. Aside from Hector and Godfrey who have picked off more than a few branches from our family tree, our lives had been pretty cat-free. And they had quit coming over entirely as soon as the Farnsworth family moved in and Boomer started patrolling the perimeter. There were the lions and tigers we had seen in the old circus posters and wagons. So basically, we had a pretty good idea of how cats generally were built. But Finnigan was turning out to be a different animal entirely.

He lost the fluffy baby fur almost right away, and what grew in was short, and sleek and smooth...kind of like the sealskin cape still hanging in Old Man Farnsworth's hall closet. His neck was really short, and his head was a little bit flat. Leroy said one day that he thought

Finnigan looked a little like a rattlesnake any time he was surprised and pinned his ears back. I told him to keep that thought to himself so that Finnigan didn't get a complex.

His legs grew to be pretty long—longer than either Hector's or Godfrey's—and it seemed like he was almost walking on stilts.

But it was his tail that really stood out. It was covered with black and grey rings down nearly the whole length, with a white tip at the end. And it was longer than the rest of him. He could wrap it around himself nearly *twice* when he curled up in a ball to take a nap in the barn, the little white tip poking up from the purring pile of fur like a lantern in the dark. When he walked across a dusty floor, it dragged behind and left a trail in the dust like a piece of rope.

Watching Finnigan nap, Leroy pondered this strange critter and his arrival in our lives.

"Where do you think he came from?" he asked.

I wondered that myself sometimes, but anything I imagined wasn't very cheerful. "I don't know, Leroy. But I think he's pretty lucky that Lucy found him and brought him back here."

"Yeah," said Leroy, picking his teeth with a piece of straw. Then he looked at me with wide eyes. "Do you think he's all cat?"

"What do you mean, 'all cat?' " Leroy could come up with the darnedest ideas. "Well...just look at that tail of his," he said. "Do you think he's part monkey?"

"What on earth makes you think that?" I asked.

Leroy pointed to the far side of the barn, which was covered with old circus posters. "There are *lots* of things in the circus that are more than one thing," he said. "That 'dragon lady' for one. And what about Marion, the mermaid?"

I peered through the gloom at the posters from long-ago side shows. Their colors had faded a long time ago, but if you used your imagination, wouldn't you think that mermaid gal really had a bright turquoise tail and was fished out of the China Sea, and that the dragon lady was born with shiny green scales.

Oh, Leroy is so gullible it's...charming some times. Just not particularly right now.

"I hate to let you down, big fella, but I'm pretty sure that the mermaid was a lady in a fish costume, and the dragon lady had fake scales and fingernails."

"Really?" he asked, looking a little sad. "I was always hoping I could see a mermaid someday."

I patted him on his big shoulder for comfort. "I would bet all the cheese in Switzerland that Finnigan is really 'all cat,' " I said. "Now let's go find something to eat."

* * * * *

Leroy and I took the little fella adventuring all over the place...as long as we could keep him out of sight of the house. Every nook and cranny in the barn, both high and low. As Finnigan's legs grew, he started to perfect his "pounce," jumping from beams to bales, and from wagons to wallboards with the ease of an acrobat. He pounced on bugs. He pounced on Boomer. He even pounced on Leroy...but gave that up when it scared Leroy so much he fainted.

When Mr. Farnsworth was off at work, we went on plenty of excursions around the yard too, and down to the stream.

If Charlie was fishing, we kept to the bushes along the banks of the stream. But Charlie started to make friends in town, so he spent more and more time away from the house on some of those long summer days. Of course with a cool place like this, sometimes all the boys ended up back here with a ruckus and a clatter and a bunch of fishing poles, so we three made ourselves scarce. We explained Fred's whole "cat allergy" thing to Finnigan right away, and how he needed to stay "under the radar" and keep from being seen. He became an absolute ninja master at blending in with the shadows in the barn.

Lucy came by to visit him every day, bringing cat food that Cindy had pilfered from Hector and Godfrey's stash at Cindy's house, and bowls of cream from the kitchen. As he got bigger and bigger, though, "borrowing" food from those evil cats was going to get noticed. And so one day Lucy and Cindy showed up with an entire bag of cat food that they bought with Lucy's allowance and hid in the barn behind the costume trunk.

If Fred Farnsworth sneezed more than he liked when he went into the barn, he chalked it up to "all that darn dust" he was kicking up while he worked. And if

Mrs. Farnsworth was a wee bit suspicious of how much time the girls were spending in the barn and how her supply of cream for her coffee always seemed to run out before her next trip to the grocery store, she didn't let on. You had to wonder, though, if she knew.

Chapter Ten

AIRBORNE!

Finnigan may have been named for the muscle-bound strongman on the poster, but he sure was fond of heights almost right off the bat. Probably that whole scene of balancing on the cannon was what set the hook. At any rate, he was a sure-footed as a mountain goat...or a mouse. With those claws and long legs of his, he could leap up the sides of the wagons and across the beams that ran from side to side under the barn roof.

He even found a patch of loose shingles big enough to squeak through for some sunbathing on the roof with me and Leroy. And once he was on the roof, it was just a few steps to the power cable running from the house to the barn. He took to it like his own personal tightrope.

We were on our way up to the roof one sunny day, in fact, when Finnigan noticed what looked a little like a swing tied up in the shadows of the roof.

"What's that?" he asked, picking his way across a beam.

"It's called a trapeze," Leroy said.

"Well how does it work"? Finnigan asked.

Leroy pointed toward a poster on the far side of the barn for "The Great Costellos" in the Sells Brothers Circus. Five guys wearing tights and spiffy mustaches were way up in the air above a crowd. One hung from a bar by his feet, another swung upside down by his knees, and one seemed to be absolutely flying fearlessly through the air toward another guy waiting to catch him by the wrists.

Leroy motioned toward the roof. He'd had a good-sized lunch of apples and walnuts, and was deeply desiring a nap in the sunlight.

"Really!" Finnigan said. "Heck, I want to try it."

"Hmmm... I said. "I think it's supposed to work better with a partner. And I think it works even better if there's a safety net under you in case you fall."

"Oh you guys just worry too much," Finnigan said, and he hopped over to the top of the ladder and began to chew at the twine that held the trapeze to the platform.

"Oh, let me help," I said. "You might chew through something important!"

Leroy just sat there and watched, his desire to rest in the sunlight balancing against curiosity about just what could happen next.

Between the two of us we got the trapeze loose. Finnigan grabbed the bar with a paw and held it close to his chest. He looked over at the poster again like it was a set of operating instructions.

Before I could even blink, he said "Watch me!" and grabbed the wooden bar with both front feet and launched himself off the platform into mid-air. Leroy looked like he was going to faint. It was getting to be a habit.

There's an old-fashioned song about a daring young lad on a flying trapeze who "swung through the air with the greatest of ease." That certainly was not Finnigan on his first try. He looked pretty dramatic when he pushed off...but after swinging a bit like the pendulum hanging in Old Man Farnsworth's grandfather clock, he finally came to a halt dangling over the center of the barn like a furry sack of potatoes.

Finnigan pulled himself up on his elbows and turned to look back at us.

"Now what?" he asked.

"You're going to need to swing yourself back to the platform," I yelled. He cocked an ear in my direction. Half a barn length might not be a great distance for a cat, but for a mouse it was quite a ways for my voice to carry. I ran along the side of the barn to get closer. This was going to be much easier said than done.

"How do I do that?" he asked. Leroy had joined me on the beam. "Got any ideas?" I asked. "Nah, you explain it to him," Leroy said. Like I had a degree in circus acrobatics. Ha!

"Try moving your back legs," I suggested. Finnigan did a little wiggle but still hung there in place. The platform on the other side of the barn was too far away to jump to, even for Finnigan. "Try wagging your tail back and forth," Leroy volunteered.

Finnigan dutifully swung his tail from side to side. Nothing much happened except that the trapeze quivered a little like it was a park swing kissed by a little summer breeze.

"C'mon guys, now what?" he said. "My arms are getting tired!"

Leroy and I looked at each other. He shrugged, but he had a worried look on his face. "Why not try the legs **and** the tail?" he volunteered.

Finnigan's back legs went one way and his tail went the other. Now he looked like a bag of potatoes trying to get mashed. The overall effect was a big wiggle that went nowhere. The bar slipped from under his elbows, and he caught himself with his paws. His sharp claws dug into the wooden bar like a set of fishing hooks, but it was going to be just a matter of time before he had to let go.

Finnigan kept on wiggling and getting nowhere. I saw that Leroy's eyes were transfixed, watching the end of Finnigan's tail, that little patch of white, whip back and forth, back and forth... "He's just like that big clock. If only someone could wind him up and get him going..." said Leroy, holding his big cheeks in his hands.

"That's it!" I said. "Leroy, sometimes you are just a genius!"

"What did I say?" he asked.

"Finnigan!" I yelled. He quit thrashing around and looked at me. "Start with your tail."

"What?"

"The tail! You're going to swing your tail, and then the tail's going to swing you." I was yelling as hard as I could to make a point.

"I tried that already," he said, and wiggled another whole body wiggle to make his point.

"No, little buddy, not quite." We were supposed to be the smart ones here, weren't we, and how could we claim to be his fairy godmothers if we couldn't figure a way out of this pickle?

"You've got to start at the very end." I said. "Take that tail of yours and wag it from front to back, front to back. And do...it...*slowly*..."

Finnigan rolled his eyes, but we hadn't steered him wrong yet so he gave it a try. First the tip started to move, like a dandelion waving back and forth in a breeze. Then the rest of the tail followed. Back and forth, back and forth, back and forth...

"Now what?" he called out, still gripping the bar with his claws. "I don't think it's working!"

But Leroy pointed, and I saw it too. The tail was wagging the cat. Rocked back and forth by the weight of his extra-long tail, Finnigan and the trapeze bar were starting to go back and forth, back and forth, in an actual one-two rhythm.

"Yes it is," I laughed. "Just feel it. And relax."

"Easy for you to say," he meowed, but when he looked back down, he saw that the floor was moving under him. More precisely, he was moving back and forth over the floor.

"Now put your hips into it!" Leroy shouted, getting into the spirit. Finnigan followed suit, letting his bottom half, then his whole body follow the swing of his tail.

Before long, he was swinging practically from one side of the barn to the other. He looked...magnificent! He looked...graceful! He looked...like his claws were about to give out!

Leroy clapped his hands over his eyes in fear, but I had a feeling that things were going to work out all right.

"Fly, Finnigan, fly!" I shouted, just as his paws slipped from the bar. He was at the end of a swoop that carried him forward, and he arced through the air like a flying squirrel, his tail straight out behind him like a rudder until he landed on the top of the King of Beasts wagon.

When Leroy realized that the sound he heard was just the graceful thump of a cat landing right side up like he should, instead of a "splat," he peeked and wiped a paw across his forehead. "Whew," he said. "The little guy had me worried there for a minute. Weren't you?"

I thought about fibbing and saying "no"...and then just shrugged. I was still breathing a little fast from all the excitement.

We should have remembered that old saying about cats always landing on their feet...but this felt more like a grand finale for a bona fide circus star. Finnigan scampered down to the floor of the barn and then looked up at us, beaming with pride. Once again, a shaft of sunlight fell on him...or maybe he decided to grab the spotlight for himself. Either way, the Farnsworth Circus Museum had a new star attraction...even if none of the humans knew it!

Chapter Eleven

HOME ALONE

After that, the bigger Finnigan got, the better he got on that old trapeze. Sometimes he swung by his front paws, and sometimes he swung from his back legs. He taught himself to launch in mid-air from the trapeze to assorted spots around the barn, dropping gracefully to the floor on his soft, springy feet, or catching on the rafters and then leaping to the top of one of the circus wagons.

He was starting to be quite the little daredevil. Sometimes he even jumped from the trapeze to the platform and then turned and hurled himself back to catch it again in mid-air as it swung back and forth. Too bad we had to keep it a secret from Fred and Shirley and the rest of the family. But there was just no telling what would happen if Fred and his allergies found out.

All three of us were sunning ourselves one day on the barn roof toward the end of the summer when we noticed Fred and Shirley start to pack things in the mini-van. And there seemed to be a *lot* of things to pack. Not a whole house full, like when they moved in. But a couple of big suitcases, and a picnic basket, and a diaper bag.

We watched as Lucy and Charlie carried out two backpacks and a big bag of dog food. Then all three kids got in one by one. First Charlie, then Lucy, then at last Donovan, all strapped into his car seat like it was a strait jacket. That kid wasn't going anywhere without permission!

Boomer was the last one in, and he jumped into the half-filled "way back" of the minivan and settled in on a blanket after turning around on it twice to make sure it was crumpled up just right.

We heard the van start and slip into gear. But then it stopped again. Lucy's door opened and she jumped out and ran to the barn.

"Lucy, what's the matter?" her mother called out through her window.

"I just forgot something in the barn," she said, and she slid the door open just a big enough crack for an eight year old girl to wiggle through.

"Finnigan," she said in a loud whisper, and quick as a flash, Finnigan left his sunning spot, squeezed past the loose shingle and practically flew down beams and bales to where Lucy stood.

Leroy and I followed, of course—we were a team, like the Three Musketeers!—but we couldn't cover ground nearly as fast as our feline friend with the extra-long legs.

Lucy squeezed Finnigan so tight it looked like his eyes would bulge out of his head, but he didn't complain or scratch. She put him down on the end of a wagon and looked him eye-to-eye.

"We're just going to Aunt Rosemary's place for the weekend," she said solemnly. "We'll be back in a couple of days." She dug deep in a pocket of her pink shorts, and set a handful of Finnigan's favorite kitty treats on the platform next to him. "Now don't you leave!" she said, and kissed him on the tip of his nose. Then she slipped back out of the barn. We heard the minivan door open and close, and then the popping sound of tires on gravel got farther and farther away.

Finnigan was just finishing the last of the treats when Leroy and I reached the ground floor. By now, Leroy was out of breath. We are just not used to that kind of high-speed scampering!

"So..." Finnigan said, wiping the last of the crumbs from his whiskers with a dainty white paw and then licking them. "What do we do now?"

Both he and Leroy looked at me like I had a plan worked out. OK, I admit I am clearly the brains of the outfit. I tried to put a thoughtful look on my face as I sat and pondered the question.

The barn was totally quiet except for the sound of a branch outside tapping against the wood siding. Even the barn door wasn't rattling in its metal track. It hadn't been this quiet since...well, since Lucy and her family moved in.

"Kinda feels like we got the place to ourselves," Leroy said, lifting himself up on his elbows.

"Sure does," Finnigan added, and I swear it looked like he was smiling. He stood up on all fours, and gave a stretch that ran from his nose to the white tip of his tail. Then he strolled over to the hole in the barn wall that served as his private entrance on the lower level.

"C'mon guys," he said. "We've got some exploring to do!"

As the last of his tail disappeared from view, Leroy looked at me and spread his hands. "What do you think we should do?" he asked. "Somebody has to keep him out of trouble!"

It was a good question. Since we'd first met Finnigan (and convinced him that we were his fairy godmothers) Leroy and I had always been in the lead. Alright, as the brains of the outfit, *I* was usually in the lead.

There had been so much to teach him at first—the best spots for hiding in the barn when Fred or Charlie happened to be there, the best hidden route down to the stream on hot summer days that kept him out of sight of the house, all the nooks and crannies of the old circus wagons and the shed. And most of all, just how important it was that he stay out of sight most of the time.

It must have been more than a wee bit frustrating for the little guy to live like that, always having to keep to the shadows when anybody but Lucy and Cindy were around. Of course, Lucy came out to the barn every day to play with him and cuddle him. And when you saw the way he pushed his head under her chin and purred when she held him, you knew that was always the very best part of his day. She brought him toys and treats and a soft blanket that she now had moved to the upper floor of the barn.

Little did she know that Leroy and I often snuggled into that blanket with Finnigan on cool nights. Hey, we were just trying to keep the little guy warm! Some nights she even managed to sneak him up to her room in her backpack when no one was watching. Those were definitely nights when Fred's sneezes really ramped up and broke up the stillness of the night. But so far he just grumbled about the place having "too much dust" and went back to sleep.

So Leroy and I stepped out of the barn and followed Finnigan into a whole new adventure.

Chapter Twelve

EXPLORERS

Finnigan was stretched out in the middle of the front yard, soaking up the sunlight and occasionally rolling over to scratch his back on the soft green grass. Framed by the red geraniums nearby, he looked as happy as a clam and as pretty as a picture.

"Hey guys, come on over," he said. "This feels wonderful!!"

I hung back along the edge of the yard, but Leroy has always been more... trusting. He waddled right over to Finnigan. Soon he was on his back as well, with his little paws up in the air, wriggling his shoulders into the grass like the cat right next to him. They made quite a pair! I figured my great-great-great-grandfather Felix was turning over in his grave at the notion of this cat-and-mouse game.

The two of them finally sat up and I joined them, keeping one eye on the sky for hawks. Safety in numbers, I thought. And we mice were always thinking about safety. Even more than we thought about food. Well, perhaps except for Leroy on occasion.

With the family gone, the place was so **quiet!!** Of course, out in the country or in a small town, it's never really silent. There's always the sound of the wind brushing through the tree leaves and the crickets and birds singing, and at night the owls hooting and the coyotes yipping.

Crows caw, tree branches rub against each other and squeak and groan. But if you ignore all that...the place was as quiet as it had been after Old Man Farnsworth died and went to the great Big Top in the sky. And he hadn't made much noise when he was alive, either.

Now, without the sound of Boomer sniffing around and the minivan coming and going and Donovan crying and the bikes clattering around the yard and Shirley calling the kids in for lunch...it felt quite peaceful. And kind of lonesome.

I was a little surprised at that.

It didn't seem to bother Finnigan though. You could tell by the way he walked straight up the front stairs to the porch and started sniffing around that he was enjoying being out in the open for a change. He hopped on to the cushioned seat of the porch swing and it started to rock back and forth.

"C'mon, guys," he said. "You should try this!" Leroy has always been a creature of comfort, and he scampered up the porch rail, over to the swing, and curled up on a soft spot of Finnigan's middle before I could even blink (or think twice). The two of them made quite a sight. I think Leroy could have stayed there all day long.

But Finnigan had more exploring to do, and before Leroy could even get his whiskers comfortable and his tail tucked in, Finnigan had jumped off the swing and started to pace around the porch, looking for a way in to the house.

"Over here," I said, and led the way to the back of the house. I normally only look for openings that are big enough for Leroy to fit through, but I remembered seeing a basement window with a broken corner. Sure enough, it was still there, and the three of us piled inside one by one. We landed on a dusty work bench, and jumped from there to the floor. The basement was damp and kind of smelly, and Leroy was halfway up the stairs to the kitchen when we noticed that Finnigan wasn't behind us. He was taking his time sniffing the basement from one end to the other.

"Hey buddy," Leroy called. "The good

stuff's upstairs. Don't you want to check if there are any leftovers left over?

Finnigan shook his head. "You guys go on ahead," he said. "This is all new to me." He leaped like a ballerina to the work bench and then to a shelf holding what looked like dusty glass jars of peaches and tomatoes from the turn of the century. "Find me something good," he said. "I won't be long."

So Leroy and I made our way to the kitchen. To our great disappointment, Fred and Shirley had emptied the trash before they left. There were no pizza crusts, no baked potato skins with cheese and green onions, no chocolate cake leftovers, no juicy corn on the cob to finish off. And there wasn't even a crumb of any sort left on the floor! Good grief, these folks were so much neater than Old

Man Farnsworth had ever been.

But...there was always the pantry. The door to the pantry was closed, but we still managed to squeeze through the gap between the floor and the door. This was more like it.

Leroy followed his nose up to an open bag of walnuts. Me, I paid a visit to a basket of apples, and started to nibble on one near the back of the basket. I mean, everybody expected a farmhouse to have mice, didn't they? And they certainly didn't expect us to starve!

When we finally left the pantry behind, there was no sign of Finnigan in the kitchen. The house was completely still except for the ticking of the grandfather clock. Leroy ran up to the kitchen table, an interesting feat since he held a bunch of walnut pieces under one arm.

"I thought I heard something," he said.

"Like what?

"I dunno," he said, and sat and took a bite of walnut. "You know, I never noticed it before, but this place is kind of pretty now." He looked around at the frilly white curtains at the window and the vase of wildflowers and geraniums sitting on the kitchen table on the red and white checkered tablecloth. "I like what they've done with the place. Don't you?"

At least that what I think he said. It sounded, with his mouth full of walnut, more like "dmmph mmph uummph?"

I climbed to the top of the table and joined him. I still couldn't hear anything but when I looked past the flowers and out the window, I thought I saw movement of some kind in the bushes by the side of the house. I squinted my eyes to see better.

"Hey fellas, what's up?" Finnigan had leaped up to land behind us on the table and I nearly jumped out of my skin.

"Don't *do* that!" I snapped a little harshly.

"I thought I heard somethin'," Leroy repeated.

"You can't always trust those big ears," I said. "It's probably nothing. Let's go check out the upstairs."

I turned to go, but then I saw that Finnigan's attention was clearly fixed on something outside the kitchen, on the other side of the glass. I looked over at Leroy, who had stopped chewing and was looking in the same direction. His eyes were about twice their usual size, and he was quivering like a bowl of Jello. I followed their gaze, and gulped.

News sure traveled fast in a small town like Beechville. With Boomer securely in the minivan and headed out of town for the weekend, Hector and Godfrey had come over to "play."

Chapter Thirteen

Uh-Oh...

O h, this means trouble," said Leroy, and he looked rather pale.

"Who are they?" Finnigan asked.

"Nobody good," I said, and shook my head.

"I haven't met these guys before. And why are they supposed to be trouble?" I noticed that the white tip of his tail was starting to twitch with curiosity. But if you've ever heard the old saying that "curiosity killed the cat," I had a feeling that the mice might come out the worse on this adventure.

"C'mon, guys," I said, and I tugged at Finnigan's elbow. "We should get out of here before they see us." Leroy and I both edged back toward the edge of the table. Finnigan kept staring out the window at Hector and Godfrey. They had stopped halfway across the yard, and Hector had his grumpy face turned up like he was sniffing the air for the scent of—what else?—mice. Godfrey just kept perfectly still beside him, a giant fluffy footstool of danger. Finnigan's tail kept twitching,

twitching, twitching... I looked over at Leroy. He seemed hypnotized.

I threw my hands up and clapped Leroy on the back. "We've gotta go. Finnigan, we'll see you back in the barn. We're going to take the high road."

"Uh huh," Finnigan grunted, not taking his eyes off the cats in the yard.

I quietly led the way to the stairs leading up to the bedrooms. Quiet as a mouse, I was, and the house seemed as silent as a tomb. Then I could hear Leroy panting and grunting behind me. His arms were full of walnuts, and another couple of walnut pieces filled out his cheeks. I stared daggers at him.

"What?" he asked, but it came out "whhhmmmmff?"

"Would you put those down!" I nearly

screeched.

He shook his head, and as he did one piece of walnut nearly fell. I caught it before it hit the floor. "This is supposed to be a quick getaway!" I hissed. "What are you thinking?"

Leroy gulped down the walnuts that were stuffed in his cheeks. "Well, Max, I'm thinking that it might be a long time before we get back to the house again until the Farnsworths come home and we ought to get in some supplies. And these walnuts are tasty!"

Ah, it was always the stomach for the big guy.

We jumped as we heard a solid "thump" in the kitchen. Finnigan had jumped off the table and was clearly on the move. I ran back to the kitchen door and peeked in, hoping that I'd find him following us up the staircase, but all I saw was the white tip of that long tail disappearing back down the stairs to the basement. Oh, it was such a lonely feeling I had right then!

I turned back to Leroy. "OK, it's just you and me, kid." I took some of the walnuts from his arms. "Let me help you." Leroy could be really, really stubborn when it came to food. I knew we could stand there all day and argue or...I could just help him out and get us back to the barn a lot faster.

We got to the top of the stairs and then left through the hole under the eaves and into the branch of the apple tree by Lucy's bedroom. We stopped short of where the branch met up with the power cable, and hid out in the leaves, watching the yard below.

Finnigan and Hector and Godfrey were sitting there, chatting like old friends. Hector and Godfrey looked really, really happy that they'd found another cat in the neighborhood. Like they'd just expanded their hunting party by one. Finnigan threw his head back and laughed at something they said—how I wished I knew what!

"What do you think they're talking about," Leroy asked with a scared little quiver in his voice.

"I don't know, buddy," I said. "I just don't know."

I noticed that every once in a while Finnigan looked up and around the trees at the edge of the yard. It seemed like he was being casual...maybe even a little too casual. Then it looked like Hector asked him a question, and Finnigan just shrugged his shoulders. The tip of his tail, though, keep twitching slightly, back and forth, back and forth. I didn't like the looks of this.

"C'mon, Leroy," I said. "We have got to get out of here and back to the barn." In my heart of hearts I had a nagging little fear that kept growing bigger. What if Leroy and I had been wrong when we took Finnigan under our wings and sold him on that "fairy godmother" story? What if all the fun the three of us had hanging out in the barn and down by the stream was just a lovely dream? What if all that he needed to turn into a ferocious, night-hunting, mouse-munching cat was meeting up with the cats up the road? Oh, I didn't want to even think about it...but part of being a mouse and staying alive is figuring out which is the safest road to travel!

The wind had started to pick up, and the branch started to shiver in the breeze. "We should leave the nuts behind," I told Leroy, and ran back to stash the ones I carried in the rain gutter. Leroy followed my lead, and then we began the journey from the safety of the tree branch to the power line that ran like a tightrope across the open yard. The line swayed faintly, but Leroy and I had crossed it a hundred times before this and I wasn't worried. I looked down. Finnigan, Hector and Godfrey still sat in their cozy conversation in the center of the yard.

Finnigan seemed raptly interested in something that Godfrey was telling him. And then all of a sudden, Godfrey gave a screech and jumped a foot in the air. When he landed, he was rubbing his nose and had a deep scowl on this face and was straight up at Leroy and me. I looked over my shoulder at Leroy.

He spread his hands and shrugged. "I thought I could tuck just a couple more walnut pieces under my arms, but one of them slipped." Then he looked down, and the evil, hungry stare radiating off of Godfrey's face caused Leroy to lose focus...and then to quiver and lose his balance. He started to wobble. And then the power cable started to wobble.

I had all I could do just to keep my own balance on the line. When I looked down, I saw that Hector was licking his chops, and Godfrey was practically bouncing up and down with excitement, positioning himself right under where Leroy would fall.

And fall he certainly would.

He had dropped the other walnut to help stay upright, but with his extra size and weight, coordination has never been one of his strong points. I watched in horror as he started to tip backwards from the power cable, keeping himself from falling by one little paw. I was too far ahead of him to reach back, so I inched backwards on the line. Just a few more inches, and I'd be there to help him.

"Hang on Leroy!" I yelled.

"I can't," he shouted back. And then he yelled, "Finnigan!!"

Chapter Fourteen

THE CIRCUS CAT

While Hector and Godfrey had been content to just sit below and wait for gravity to deliver Leroy for their dinner, Finnigan had been pacing back and forth below us, his tail cracking back and forth like a lion tamer's whip. Then, as Leroy began to topple dangerously, Finnigan launched himself up the side of the apple tree, claws digging in like iron boat hooks. In a blink, he was up the tree and on the branch, heading straight for the power cable where Leroy held on for dear life. But when Finnigan's weight landed on the branch, it jiggled the cable some more, and Leroy, dear Leroy, could just not hold on any longer.

I squeezed my eyes tightly shut, but not before I saw, like it was in slow motion, Leroy start to fall through the air. And then I saw Finnigan flying sideways through the air to meet him.

I waited for the sure-to-come sound of Leroy hitting the ground, but instead, I found myself riding a wave. That cable had absolutely come to life and was jerking up and down like a trampoline.

I looked, and couldn't believe my eyes. Finnigan had caught Leroy in mid-air, and was holding him in his front paws like a baby rocking in a cradle. Leroy was looking up at Finnigan with a mixture of shock and pure gratitude. Hector and Godfrey were looking up at Finnigan like he was an alien that had just landed from outer space. And when my eyes followed the length of Finnigan from the paws that held Leroy to the end of him, my jaw fell wide open in surprise.

That tail of his had saved the day. That wonderful, long, ridiculous tail. Finnigan was hanging by his tail like a monkey as the wind swayed the two of them back and forth, the tail coiled around the cable like picture wire on the back of a painting, the rest of the cat floating back and forth, free in the breeze. And better yet, Finnigan looked like he was enjoying himself!

Godfrey hissed furiously. Hector spat and leaped straight up, like he was trying to reach Finnigan and Leroy, but fell far short. Finnigan just laughed.

"Sorry, fellas," he called back. "These guys are family!"

He hung there for a few seconds more as Hector and Godfrey exchanged hissy fits. I'll never know what would have happened next, because at that moment, the Farnsworths drove back into the yard.

As the van pulled to a stop, the back hatch flew open. Boomer jumped out, uttered a rare and thunderous "WOOF!!" and chased Hector and Godfrey out of the yard and into the woods. It sounded like a cannonball was crashing through the forest, with branches cracking and small trees bending, and the occasional screech and hiss when Boomer got close to the fleeing cats.

As the rest of the Farnsworths piled out of the minivan, Finnigan swung his weight back and forth to get a little momentum. Then he grabbed Leroy in his teeth by the back of his neck, just like a mother cat would do for her kitten, while he managed to catch the cable with his feet. He continued the overhead route and tiptoed across the rest of the cable to the roof of the barn and out of sight of the yard just as Fred Farnsworth stepped out of the van and stretched, looking up at the sky.

"Well, here's to Aunt Rosemary having the mumps," he said. "We'll just have to try to visit again some other weekend."

Then he drew his handkerchief out of his back pocket and launched into a trio of sneezes as deep as the Grand Canyon.

Boomer came trotting back into the yard, a few burrs stuck to his sides but with a victorious and happy look on his face. Fred patted him on the head. "Well, I guess that solves the question of whether we have any cats around here—not with you on duty, big fella!"

Shirley laughed as she dug the little guy out of his car seat. "See honey, I told you there were no cats to worry about!" Donovan frowned when he heard that and pointed toward the top of the barn, making "ka...ka...ka..." sounds.

Shirley turned and looked up at the apple tree. Two blackbirds took flight from the branches just as Finnigan and I made it to the eaves of the barn roof and hid in the shadows.

"You saw a crow?" she asked. "Very good, Donovan, very good!" And she patted his head as she walked up the porch stairs and carried him into the kitchen.

Chapter Fifteen

A CIRCUS FAMILY

Back in the barn, Finnigan set Leroy—who was both walnut-less and had fainted from the shock of his rescue—on a sunny pile of hay to warm up. I sat beside him, holding his paw, and fanning him until he woke up.

At the creak of the barn door opening, Finnigan flew to his special nest of blankets and curled up as though he had been asleep for the entire afternoon. Lucy burst through the door and raced to his hiding place. She picked him up and hugged him tightly.

"I'm so glad we're back!!" she said. "You must have been so bored and *lonesome* here all alone! I'm going to bring you some extra treats tonight to make up for it."

Then she skipped back to the house to unpack, and we again had the barn to ourselves.

The word "treats" had brought Leroy right back to wide awake, and we both scooted over to share Finnigan's blanket with him.

He looked at us with a twinkle in his eye. "Bored?" he said.

"I think if I get any more bored, I'll die of a heart attack," I replied, and I meant every word.

Leroy cuddled up against Finnigan's shoulder. "Thanks for the rescue, Finn," he said. "I thought I was a goner for sure."

"Well, when I saw you start to fall, I thought you were too!" Finnigan licked a stray wild hair from Leroy's forehead, and started to purr. "I knew it was going to take more than magic to get you out of trouble back there."

Leroy looked up at him with a frown on his face. "What do you mean?" he asked carefully.

Finnigan laughed. "I've been on to this

whole fairy godmother thing for a while," he said.

"But how did you know?" Leroy looked confused.

"Guys, Lucy has been reading me enough fairy tales to figure out that if I really had a fairy godmother, she would look more like me!"

What a day of surprises! I just had to know. "So how long were you on to us?" I asked.

"Let's just say longer than you would expect," Finnigan said, and he grinned.

Leroy looked confused and a little embarrassed. He looked up at his rescuer. "So why didn't you say anything? We must have sounded pretty silly," he said.

Finnigan gave him a little squeeze with

one snowy white paw. "I figured having you two were the closest thing I had to family, and family is way more important than fairy tales," he said.

"You had me a little worried there when we first saw you with Hector and Godfrey," I admitted. "I didn't what was going to happen next, or if you were going to decide to hang out with a pair of thugs like them just because you're a cat too."

Finnigan's eyebrows shot up at that, and Leroy looked at me like I had started speaking Martian. "How could you think anything like that," he said. "We're a family here! Not just a family, but a circus family!"

I took a long look around the barn, at the wagons and the posters and the trapeze and the cannon. And the air around me felt full of all the memories and spirits of the circus folk and circus animals (and particularly circus mice!) that had come before me and Leroy.

Of Finnigan the Strongman, and Old Man Farnsworth. Of our great-great-great grandfather Felix who used to be the royal doctor's "pocket mouse" until the lights in the circus tent and the smell of the sawdust in Berlin proved too strong to resist.

Of the clowns and the acrobats and the bearded ladies and the human cannonballs who wowed crowds and made children laugh and grownups gasp as they did their tricks and worked their magic.

Over the years and over the centuries, folks who had stuck together like glue, and like family. Not only because some of them were born into the circus life, but because they all found a magic there, and an energy, and an enchantment that bound them together in ways stronger than just a family name or sharing a house.

I still think that I'm the brains of the outfit, but sometimes...just sometimes... Leroy manages to hit the nail right on the head.

I picked out a patch of Finnigan's side to lean up against, and put my hands behind my head, enjoying the warmth of his coat and the purr rumbling from inside it. He snaked that long, furry tail of his around himself a time and a half and snuggled both Leroy and me a little closer inside its coils.

"Leroy," I admitted, "you couldn't be more right than that. We are absolutely a circus family in the long tradition of circus families...and Finnigan has proven he is most *definitely* a circus cat!"

Finnigan reached across Leroy and licked me on the forehead. "Shhhh...." he said. "I think I finally could use a nap."

Then the three of us drifted off to sleep, dreaming of the circus, and magic, and the center ring.

Mary T. Wagner is an award-winning author and essayist in Wisconsin.

She first started to imagine the story about Finnigan the Circus Cat after her younger son and his wife brought home the smallest kitten she had ever seen from an animal shelter. The wee little Finnigan thrived with large doses of cuddles and cream, and is still the source of limitless laughs for Mary and her family. Finnigan now has a "little brother" named Linus, who is ALSO a rescue kitten.

Coming soon...!!

FINNIGAN

and

THE LOST CIRCUS WAGON

When the Farnsworths acquire a broken-down old circus wagon for the family circus museum, nobody knows that it really comes with a valuable secret.

Nobody in Beechville, that is. But when two shady characters come to town with plans to steal it away, it's up to Finnigan, Max and Leroy to send them packing!